JR. CHAPTER BOOK

THE
BAILEY SCHOOL
KIDS

1

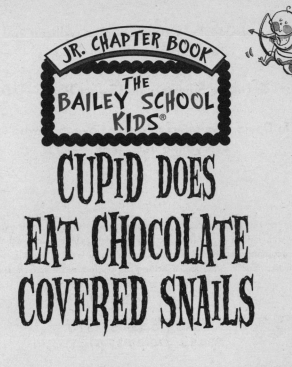

JR. CHAPTER BOOK

THE BAILEY SCHOOL KIDS®

CUPID DOES EAT CHOCOLATE COVERED SNAILS

by Marcia Thornton Jones and Debbie Dadey
Illustrated by Joëlle Dreidemy

SCHOLASTIC INC.
New York Toronto London Auckland Sydney
Mexico City New Delhi Hong Kong Buenos Aires

To two of Cupid's favorite couples: Allison and Will, and Jared and Lisa!—M.J.

To Deidre Summerville (Sweet Pea).—D.D.

To David, a wonderful Mister Lovegood who loves everything but...pink! — J.D.

ISBN-10: 0-439-87631-1
ISBN-13: 978-0-439-87631-5

Text copyright © 2007 by Marcia Thornton Jones and Debra S. Dadey.
Illustrations copyright © 2007 by Scholastic Inc.
All rights reserved. Published by Scholastic Inc.

SCHOLASTIC and associated logos are trademarks and/or registered trademarks of Scholastic Inc.

12 11 10 9 8 7 6 5 4 3 2 1   7 8 9 10 11 12/0

Printed in the U.S.A.
First printing, January 2007

CONTENTS

1
STRIKE

"Strike!" Melody yelled. Melody and Liza jumped up and down at the bowling alley.

"Look," Liza said. "Your name is in lights." Above their heads, red lights flashed showing that Melody's ball had knocked down all the pins.

Eddie's grandmother had taken Eddie, Howie, Melody, and Liza to the Bailey City Bowling Alley as a surprise for Valentine's Day. Eddie's grandmother loved to bowl. She bowled every Wednesday in a league. Sometimes she brought Eddie with her, but this was the first time she had taken his friends along.

Eddie's grandmother left them for a few minutes while she went to the snack bar to buy treats. Eddie was hoping that she would bring back french fries!

"I can get a strike too!"
Eddie bragged. "Just watch."
Eddie stepped up to the line,
holding a blue bowling ball in
front of him.

He took a running start and
tossed the ball.
"*Awwwww!*" Eddie
screamed. He slid down the
lane with the ball still stuck to
his thumb.

"Are you all right?" asked
a strange voice.
Eddie looked up. He
couldn't believe what he saw.

2

PINK NUT

Eddie had never seen so much pink. Pink shoes. Pink pants. Pink shirt. Pink skin. Even pink hair! The pink man held a pink hand out to Eddie.

"Are you okay?" the man asked again.

Melody came up beside the pink man. "Eddie's fine," she said. "He falls down all the time."

The pink man walked away carrying three bowling balls in his big, pink arms. He juggled the three heavy balls as if they weighed nothing.

"Did you see that?" Howie asked.

Melody nodded. "I saw a woman with pink hair once. It looked like she had cotton candy on her head."

"What kind of nut has pink hair and juggles bowling balls?" Eddie asked.

Melody pointed to the man. He had put down the balls and was helping Eddie's grandmother carry the snacks.

"A very nice nut," Melody said.

15

3

MR. LOVEGOOD

"Why, thank you, Mr. Lovegood," Eddie's grandmother said as they walked up carrying armloads of popcorn, hot dogs, and soft drinks. "You came JUST in time!"

Mr. Lovegood put his tray on a table. "I aim to please," he said before bowing low to the ground.

Eddie's grandmother giggled and smoothed down her gray curls. "Oh, my," she said. "Such a gentleman. May I offer you a snack?" she asked, holding her tray out to him.

"No thanks, I have my own," Mr. Lovegood said, pulling a small box from his pocket. "Would you like some?"

Eddie's grandmother read the box label. "Chocolate-covered snails. I've never tried those. Thank you."

Liza stared in horror as Eddie's grandmother and Mr. Lovegood popped the snails into their mouths.

Even Eddie,
who loved candy,
stuck out his tongue.

Blech!

He held
his throat.

Yuck!

He fell to
the floor.

Ugh!

Mr. Lovegood reached into
his other pocket and pulled out
a roll of stickers.

He plucked a sticker off the
roll and gently put it on Eddie's
grandmother's collar. "You might
enjoy bowling with Mr. Oswell
for a while," he said.

Then Mr. Lovegood rushed over three lanes and plopped a sticker on a bald-headed man. As soon as the sticker hit his head, Mr. Oswell dropped his bowling ball with a thud and smiled at Eddie's grandmother.

Eddie's grandmother did the unthinkable. She dropped her tray of snacks and hurried over to meet Mr. Oswell.

SPLAT went the hot dogs on the floor.

SPLAT!

SPLAT went the soft drinks on the floor.

DRAT

"DRAT!" went Eddie, looking at the ruined snacks.

Eddie's grandmother didn't watch the kids bowl for the rest of the day. She didn't see Howie knock down all his pins. She didn't see Liza finally get the ball all the way down the lane. Instead, Eddie's grandmother watched Mr. Oswell.

4

STICKERS

"This is great," Eddie said. "Grandma isn't paying attention. I can get away with ANYTHING!"

Eddie's grandmother was so busy bowling with Mr. Oswell, she didn't watch Eddie put two straws in his mouth and squirt soda all over Melody.

Hey!

She didn't see Eddie take all the bowling balls from the kids beside them.

She didn't even pay attention when he hula-danced down the lane.

"Eddie, behave!" Liza warned him.

"Why?" Eddie wanted to know.

"Because it's the right thing to do," Melody said. "Besides, you could get in trouble."

"Grandma's not even looking," Eddie told his friends. "I can do anything I want."

"She usually watches you like a teacher giving a test," Howie said.

"It is strange," Liza said. "Ever since Mr. Lovegood gave her that snail she's been acting funny."

CRUNCH CRUNCH

"I still can't believe they ate snails," Melody said, holding her belly. "It's so yucky."

"People eat lots of strange things," Howie said. "Like worms, ants, and even grasshoppers."

"That's sick!" Liza said.

"I ate a bug once," Eddie admitted. "It was big and creepy and crawly."

Liza covered her mouth.

"Don't listen to Eddie," Melody said. "Maybe it isn't the snails at all. That sticker could have made your grandmother act so funny."

The four friends looked at Eddie's grandmother. "What's on that sticker, anyway?" Howie asked.

 "It's a heart with an arrow through it," Melody said.

"Uh-oh," said Howie, pointing down the lanes. Mr. Lovegood plopped stickers on two teenagers.

As soon as he did, the two kids smiled and then held hands.

"I think we have a problem," Howie said. "A very sticky problem!"

5

CUPID

"You guys are not going to believe this," Howie said.

"What's wrong?" Liza asked.

"Shh," Howie put his finger to his lips. He whispered to his friends, "I think Mr. Lovegood is some kind of love creature."

"Are you crazy?" Eddie asked.

Melody tossed her black braids out of her face and asked, "Do you mean like Cupid?"

"Don't be silly," Eddie said. "Cupid flies around shooting people with love arrows. I'm pretty sure the bowling alley doesn't allow arrows."

Howie nodded. "That's why he's using stickers to make people fall in love."

"That's gross," Eddie said with a shudder. The word love made Eddie feel a little sick.

"It's actually kind of sweet," Liza said. "Just think how nice the world would be if everyone loved one another."

Eddie shook his head. "It would not be nice. It would be icky. My grandmother is not in love and I'll prove it."

6

MAD

Liza tried to stop Eddie. She jumped in front of him, but Eddie walked around her. She grabbed his elbow, but Eddie jerked away. She even tried to tackle him, but ended up with her face in a box of popcorn instead.

SPLAT!

Eddie walked right up to his grandmother. "Are you in love?" he asked.

Liza gasped and Melody held her breath, but Eddie's grandmother didn't even hear him. "Not now, Eddie. I'm watching Mr. Oswell knock down all those pins."

While Mr. Oswell waited for his ball to return, he offered Eddie's grandmother a big candy bar. Eddie held out his hand, sure that his grandmother would give him a piece. She didn't. Instead, she giggled and shared it with Mr. Oswell.

35

"What's she doing?" Eddie
asked. "Why didn't she give
me any? She knows I love
chocolate." Eddie frowned. He
loved any kind of candy. Big.
Little. Sweet. Sour.

It didn't matter to Eddie,
as long as it wasn't snails.

"I think she is falling in
love," Melody said.

"No!" Eddie snapped.
He wanted that candy and he
wanted it now.

Eddie crossed
his arms.

He stomped his foot.

He was so mad, he didn't
notice what was heading his
way.

"Eddie!" Melody
squealed. "Watch out!"

7

ESCAPE

Eddie turned around and ran right into a pink wall. Actually it wasn't a wall at all, it was Mr. Lovegood!

"I have a little surprise for you," Mr. Lovegood said. "You're going to LOVE it!" He held out a sticker toward Eddie.

"NOOOOOOOOOOOO!"
screamed Eddie.

He fell over a chair.

He hopped across a lane.

He dodged a rolling
bowling ball.

"RUN!" Eddie yelled to his
friends. "Run for your lives."

The four kids darted between bowlers. They raced to the snack bar. They dived under tables and chairs.

"Why are we running?" Liza asked as she tried to catch her breath. "Mr. Lovegood was only trying to be nice."

The four kids stopped running. Eddie started to answer Liza. But he didn't have a chance because just then someone tapped him on the shoulder.

Eddie turned around.
A girl with curly blond hair
squeezed his arm.
It was Carey from
their second-grade
class.

Carey batted
her eyelashes at Eddie.
"I've been looking for you,"
she said.

"Looking for me?" Eddie
asked. "Why?"

"Because," Carey said in a too-sweet voice. "I thought we could bowl together."

"Bowl?" Eddie repeated. "Together?"

When Carey nodded her curls bounced. "Just you and me," she said.

"He can't bowl with you," said a voice from behind Eddie. "He's going to bowl with ME."

Eddie turned around to see Izzy. Everyone knew Izzy because she had a pet parrot. Today, the parrot was sitting on top of Izzy's head.

Izzy grabbed Eddie's other arm. "He's mine," she said.

"Is not," Carey said, pulling Eddie one way.

"Is too," Izzy argued, yanking Eddie the other way.

"Not," yelled Carey, tugging on Eddie's arm.

"Too," Izzy shouted.

With that, Izzy pulled so
hard that Eddie went flying
through the air.

"Save me!" Eddie yelled.
Melody and Liza helped Eddie
up.

"Uh-oh," Howie said. "Do
you see what I see?"

Gulp!

9

GIRLS

Big girls. Little girls. Girls of every size and shape were headed straight toward them.

"Isn't he cute?" one said. "I saw him first," another one said.

"He's mine!" Izzy told them.
"No, he's mine!" Carey
screamed.

"Who cares about Eddie?"
a short girl said. "I like Howie!"
Another girl pushed the first
girl aside. "I like him more than
you do!"

"Me?" Howie said with
a grin. "You like me?"

"Don't be too glad,"
Melody said. "Those girls are
crazy. Crazy in love, thanks to
Mr. Lovegood."
While the girls yelled at
each other, Melody and Liza
pulled Howie and Eddie away.

"Melody is right," Liza said.
"Mr. Lovegood is Cupid and
he's made all the girls fall in
love with you."

"He can't be Cupid. Cupid
wouldn't eat snails," Howie
said.

"In Bailey City, Cupid DOES eat chocolate-covered snails, and if we don't stop him there's going to be trouble. Love trouble," Melody told him.

It was true. All the girls at the bowling alley wore heart stickers from Mr. Lovegood.

Eddie gulped. "We have to get rid of those stickers," he said.

"You can't," Melody said.

"Why not?" Eddie asked.

"Because you and Howie are going to be running from those girls," Liza said.

A huge mob of girls raced toward Eddie and Howie. Eddie took one look and screamed. Howie jumped and raced toward the boys' bathroom. "Wait for me!" Eddie yelled.

10

LOVE WARS

"We have to help Eddie and Howie," Liza said. "But what can we do?"

Melody jumped up and down. "I know. We can grab all those heart stickers and tear them into little pieces."

Liza gasped. "That's not nice."

"We have to do it," Melody said. "Look around." Girls were pounding on the boys' bathroom door. Mr. Oswell and another man were shoving each other as they tried to get to Eddie's grandmother. The snack bar worker tipped over a tub of popcorn as he reached over the counter to hug a lady.

All over the bowling alley, the girls heard people yelling things like, "I saw him first," and "I love her more than you."

"Okay," Liza said. "Let's do it!"

"Operation Get Stickers starts in five, four, three, two, one, GO!" Melody yelled.

Melody raced to the
girls. She ripped off all of their
stickers before they knew what
happened.

"Excuse me," Liza said
politely to all the older men and
women before snatching their
stickers. "Please forgive me."

Melody waited until Mr. Lovegood had swallowed a chocolate snail before grabbing the stickers from his hand.

"Sorry," she yelled. "But we have to save our friends."

Melody and Liza quickly tore the stickers into little pieces. "We did it!" Liza squealed.

"But did it work?" Melody asked.

Melody and Liza looked around. The girls stopped pounding on the boys' bathroom door. Their faces turned as red as a Valentine heart when they realized where they were.

Mr. Oswell and the other man stopped pushing each other. They shook hands and sat down to wipe the sweat from their foreheads.

The snack bar worker tripped on the spilled popcorn and landed on the seat of his pants.

All over the bowling alley, people were saying things like, "I'm so sorry" and "Please forgive me."

Eddie and Howie creeped out of the bathroom.

"We tore up all the stickers," Liza told the boys.

"Thanks," Eddie said.

Howie nodded. "That was scary."

Eddie's grandmother came back to the kids. Her face looked a little green. "Sorry to be gone so long," she said. "I'm not sure what came over me. Maybe it was that funny candy from Mr. Lovegood. I'm never eating those again."

"Good idea," Eddie said. "In Bailey City, one thing is for sure, Cupid DOES eat chocolate-covered snails!"